MW01251821

When Leaves Fall

A Different Point of View Story

By

C. A. King

**Cover Design:
Just Write Creations**

Editor: J.D. Cunegan

To Linda
Happy Reading
Clak

Dedication & Acknowledgement

*This book is dedicated to Biscuit - my faithful
companion lost to cancer in 2015
Always in my heart.*

Look for other Books by C.A. King including:

The Portal Prophecies:
Book I - A Keeper's Destiny
Book II - A Halloween's Curse
Book III – Frost Bitten
Book IV - Sleeping Sands
Book V – Deadly Perceptions

Book VI – Finding Balance

Tomoiya's Story:

Book I: Escape to Darkness

Book II: Collection Tears

Surviving the Sins:

Book I: Answering the Call

Cover Design: **Just Write Creations**

First Printing: 2017

ISBN 978-1-988301-16-7

Kings Toe Publishing
kingstoepublishing@gmail.com
Burlington, Ontario. Canada

Chapter One

The vision in his left eye took a few minutes to begin to clear. Not that it mattered much - everything was dark. The floor was cold - no, not floor - dirt. He was lying on dirt. He surveyed the situation from where his head was positioned - not wanting to move. Wherever he was, it was unfamiliar.

He squinted, trying to focus. His eyesight wasn't what it used to be when he was younger. For that matter, nothing was the same as it was when he was younger. For all intents and purposes, he was old. The blurriness that came hand-in-hand with age dissipated enough to at least look around a little.

A shack. He was in a shack made entirely out of wood and poorly at that. Whoever built it must have had minimal skills with a hammer and saw. From where he lay, it seemed quite possible the whole roof was slanted. One thing was for sure, the structure wasn't very big - maybe twice the size of him lying down and a bit taller than him standing up. There were spaces between the planks of wood that formed the walls. A wind storm would most likely make quick work of the place.

An exit. There was definitely a doorway, although he couldn't see a door. It was more a large gap - as if someone had meant to put a door on and never got around to doing it. Still, it was a way out.

His heart raced at the thought of leaving the shack. There was an unnatural feeling in the pit of his stomach that screamed that the place was all wrong. He didn't belong there - no one did.

Home. He wanted to go home. He wanted to leave this place and never think about it again. Would he ever see his home again? He pushed the strange thought from his mind, not allowing it any time to fester and infect his will.

Once on his feet, he raced for the opening. A rattling noise came from behind him, urging him to move faster. Whatever it was making the noise could stay where it was. He had no intentions of a confrontation, especially in a place he didn't recognize. Fighting wasn't his strong suit. Through most of his life there hadn't been the need for violence. One glance at his physique had been enough to scare off anyone looking to challenge him. Of course, he hadn't been in that position in years. He wasn't sure his build was enough to send anyone running in fear anymore. Why wasn't he younger? If he was, this scenario would be playing out quite differently.

He made it outside. *Freedom.* He breathed deeply, examining his surroundings.

A house - it looked familiar. Yes, he definitely recognized it. He darted forward. Jerking backwards, he gagged and fell to the ground. His neck ached from being pulled like a puppet on a string - a string wrapped around its neck that is.

Glancing over his shoulder, he understood. It was his movements that had made the noise earlier. He was chained to the strange shed. But why? He gasped for air - suddenly realizing how tight the metal around his throat was. It had to be at least one size too small.

None of this made sense. He tried to remember what happened, but memories failed him, providing only quick glimpses of random pictures in his mind. Someone had put him there, but he didn't know who. He shivered. It was getting cold.

A bed. He remembered a warm bed covered with pillows and blankets. That's where he belonged - not lying on dirt. What did he do to deserve this? Why would anyone want to hurt him? Surely it wasn't his family.

A family. He most definitely had a family - not that he could visualize them at the moment, but he was sure they existed. He also knew they loved him as much as he loved them. His family would notice he was missing. They would come for him. He only needed to wait. He was sure they would find him.

A drop hit his nose. *Rain.* It was just his luck. He hated the rain. It was cold and wet - two things he could do without. The light

4

drizzle became heavier. Before long, the clouds opened up and a downpour pelted down on the ground and his head.

Now he was wet, cold and muddy. He screamed, hoping someone would hear him. They had to. No one deserved to be kept like this. It was obviously a mistake. Time passed. His screams continued, but no one came.

The rain slowed - amounting to little more than a misting, but the damage was already done. He was drenched. He could feel a pain in his leg from the accident he had been in a few years back - arthritis perhaps. Probably flaring up from sitting on the cold ground combined with the shower he hadn't wanted to take.

He turned to the shelter. At least inside it would be a little drier. He limped back to the opening.

Pain.

He fell to the ground. Something hit him in the back. The first blow stung, causing him to cry out. The next one was accompanied with a burning pain.

"Shut up, Ralph!" a man's voice yelled.

He felt another pelt from behind - it was definitely an object that was coming down on him, but he didn't know what it was. His eyes closed. Visions of his family danced in his head. It was a blurry picture void of detail - still it was his happy place. His family would come for him. They would save him. They had to.

Chapter Two

A grumbling in his stomach woke him. He was hungry - not just wanting something good to eat, but downright famished. He tried to stand, failing on the first attempt.

He winced at the pain radiating from his back. Flashbacks from the previous night made him cringe. Who was that man that hit him? What had he hit him with? What had he done to make a stranger so angry? He sighed. Wondering wasn't about to provide any answers.

Managing no more than a crawl, he made his way to the opening. He poked his head out first, making sure no one was going to attack before inching out slowly into the open.

The sun was up, but it wasn't warm. Remnants of leftover rain dripped off the roof of the shelter onto his head. He shook it off.

Alone. There was no one to be seen. He was alone, but somehow doubted he was safe. It didn't matter much anyways. It was a stupid mistake, but he had forgot the chain only allowed him to move so far forward. He was trapped. He tugged with all his might - only managing to tire himself out. There was no doubt about it. He was a prisoner - but jailed for what? He glanced around.

A garden. He was in a garden of some sort. There were bushes and flowers that surrounded the shed and blocked most of his view of the house in the distance. Was that his house? It couldn't be. His family wouldn't allow him to be locked up like this. Not to mention that man - even with his clouded memories, he knew the man wasn't part of his family. What had the stranger said?

Ralph. Yes - that was his name. Whoever he was, the man obviously knew him. Why didn't Ralph recognize anything about the stranger?

His stomach let out another growl. He caught a scent in the wind. Someone nearby was cooking. Food had always been one of his favourite things. He wasn't a picky eater. Just about anything would do. New memories surfaced - a table filled with foods of every type. He drooled at the thought a plate topped with a mound of multiple different types of meats and breads. He even wanted the peas and carrots he usually left behind.

Using his tongue, he sucked back in his own saliva. The little bits of spittle were barely enough to wet his mouth. He was thirsty. He looked at a puddle of rain water that was just within his reach. It was brown from the dirt, but better than nothing. He drank until it almost vanished - hoping it would not only quench his growing thirst, but hold off the hunger pains a bit as well.

He moved back inside the only shelter he had and curled up in a ball. *Waiting.* His family would come soon. They would save him from this nightmare.

He closed his eyes wondering what he had done and why someone wanted to hurt him.

Chapter Three

He heard a rustling outside the shack. Someone was there. He froze. What if it was the man again - back to beat him mercilessly? Then again, maybe it was his family.

Ralph sighed. He knew in his heart it wasn't. If it was his family, they'd be calling out for him, not sneaking around.

He put his head back down. If he yelled, he was sure he'd be hit again. It would be better to stay quiet, at least until he found out what it was the man wanted. He had been sure to keep his noise to a minimum so as not to anger the stranger. Somehow, he wasn't sure it mattered. He figured the man would be angry with him no matter what he did.

Scraps of food pelted down around him as if falling from the sky. He sniffed at a piece of fat and grizzle. *Yuck!*

Ralph was used to good food. A nice juicy steak cooked medium-raw would have been perfect to satisfy his growing appetite. His tongue darted out, licking his mouth at the thought. He glanced down at the bits of unwanted food - discarded for him to eat. There was no plate - just the dirt floor.

His hunger raged. It was less than an hour before he couldn't take it anymore. He pushed a piece of the meat, flicking off a couple of ants. If they weren't picky, he couldn't be either.

He chomped down several times on the piece before swallowing it whole. It wasn't as bad as he had thought. He moved on to another bit. Every bite, he remembered the taste of the juicy steak he had at the family barbeque. If he thought hard enough about it, he could almost taste it. It at least made swallowing this stuff easier.

He cried. His family must be looking for him. They must have noticed he was gone by now. They would come and save him. He knew they would.

Ralph lay back down, wanting to curl up again, but the pain in his leg was growing stronger by the hour. He stretched it out as flat as he could to alleviate cramps.

How long had he been there? He certainly didn't know. Time seemed to slow to a crawl in that place.

He was tired. It didn't matter that he had nothing else to do but lie around. Sleep meant forgetting. If he could sleep the whole time, he wouldn't feel so sad - or wonder what he did to deserve being chained up like he was. There was no rhyme or reason to it.

There must be a reason. If he could only remember, maybe he could make it better. Maybe he could beg for forgiveness - someone would have pity on him, especially at his age.

He whimpered, hoping the man wouldn't hear, but someone else would.

Chapter Four

Ralph had given up trying to keep track of how long he had been there. The days passed much as they had in the beginning of his imprisonment. He slept away most of his time - only getting up to eat scraps that had been thrown to him and glance around occasionally, making a note of his surroundings.

It was late fall. Leaves covered the ground. He remembered his younger days - jumping in piles of the mixed colours. In those days life had been good. He played most of the time. How easily he had taken that life for granted - believed it would always be like that. Cruel reality was setting in. He might never enjoy life again.

A single falling leaf grabbed Ralph's attention. It fluttered playfully about, caught in a gust of wind. It blew around in circles a few times before drifting peacefully down to join the others. How lucky that leaf was. If, at that exact moment, he could chose to be anything, it would have been that leaf. Ralph sighed - brought back to reality by another problem he didn't want to face.

He had chosen a corner outside the door as far away as possible to use as a bathroom. It wasn't his first choice to do his business, being so close to where he was chained up, but when one has to go, one has to go. The smell, however, was growing by the day. Of course, it was lucky it was cooler in the fall and the flies weren't out. If it had been summer the stench alone would have been too much to handle.

He wasn't sure why he had thought someone would at least clean it up. It just seemed like it was the thing to do - especially since he knew he was close to other people. He could hear them sometimes. In between naps, he made out a timetable of activity in the area. If opportunity arose for escape, he'd jump at it.

Timetables. It came back to him like a strong revelation. A schedule was something he was familiar with. His family had them. They all kept a strict routine. Now that he was older, he wasn't always able to go with them, but he knew they came and went daily. If they were going to be gone a long time, they would have someone come in to prepare his meals and take care of his needs.

The stranger had a schedule as well. He left at the exact same time every day and returned at the same time every evening.

A few times he tried to scream for help when he heard voices nearby, but no one ever responded. No matter how loud he got, it was as if no one ever heard him or if they did they didn't care. Until that day...

He had given up yelling and laid back down when he heard the stranger. The words were mumbled at first, but Ralph knew from the tone the man was angry about something.

"What's this I hear you have been making a racket all day?" he yelled. "No one wants to hear you! Do you understand me?"

Ralph backed up, shaking. A cigarette butt still lit hit him in the face, burning his nose. He winced, closing his watering eyes. The next sight Ralph had was of a shoe in the man's hand. That must have been what hit him before.

A shoe - a stupid shoe of all things.

Shoe or not, it hurt when it came down on his back again. Ralph cried out, not knowing how much more abuse he could handle. The pain was real - almost equaling the constant throbbing in his leg. The more he cried, the more the man hit.

He wanted to fight back, but what chance did he have? The stranger was large and frightened him. Ralph knew the man was strong - too strong to be overcome easily.

He had been strong once - when he was younger. He was proud of how strong he had been - strong enough to protect his whole family. That was many moons ago. He couldn't protect himself from a squirrel now - most definitely not from this man.

He backed down in silence, accepting the punishment for whatever crime he had committed. Whatever it was, it must have been horrible. Why else would he be kept like this?

Chapter Five

He remained quiet for several days. There was no use annoying the man any further. Ralph grew weaker by the day - his aches grew stronger. He tried to remember something happy, but doubt reared its ugly head. What if his memories were merely dreams of the life he wanted rather than truth of what once was?

He didn't know anymore. It was becoming harder to focus as the hands of time ticked the hours away. Was he losing his sanity?

Of course you are! How couldn't you be?

No one deserved to be confined like this. It was cruel. How could anyone do this to another living creature? No one could survive living like this. He knew he was no exception.

He could feel death breathing down his neck. Its grasp radiated through his bones. It would come for him one way or another. At this point, Ralph wasn't sure he minded. Pain and loneliness were his only companions.

He didn't know if they were real or not, but he would have given anything to spend at least a little while with that family he sometimes thought of before he took his last breath.

He had been so sure they would come for him - find him - save him. How could he have been so wrong?

Maybe he'd be better off ending things sooner. Next time the man came, maybe he should try to fight back. The man would either let him go or beat him for the last time. Either way, it didn't matter; he'd get in a good swat or two before it was over. He fell asleep content with a plan he knew he couldn't execute. He had never hurt a fly before and that wasn't about to change.

*****

He howled. A sharp pain radiated from his back leg. He caught a glimpse of a stick and

22

lunged at it. He had only meant to stop it from coming down on his leg again, but he missed - toppling over a young boy.

The two exchanged glances. The boy on his backside and Ralph now sitting up.

Another person. Ralph called out, hoping the boy would understand and get help or maybe even set him free. It didn't work.

The boy's only response was a scream. He was frightened by all of this - maybe even as much as Ralph was. Tears flowed down his small face. He scooted backwards, trying to move away. The colour drained from his face, as if he were looking into the eyes of a monster.

Ralph didn't know what to do. What he did know was, where there was a boy, there was likely to be a parent. If he could get an adult's attention, maybe he could get some help. He continued to scream as loud as he possibly could. This was his last chance someone would come. Someone would save him. The boy scrambled to his feet and bolted away, his small frame shaking in fear. Ralph watched him trip a few times before disappearing out of sight.

Of course the child was scared. Who wouldn't be seeing the conditions Ralph was forced to live in? If he made it out of there alive, he'd give that boy a big hug and kiss to make up for it.

He heard voices in the distances. If he could hear them, they most definitely could hear him. He continued to scream until his voice wouldn't make another sound.

Exhausted, he flopped down. As his eyes closed he saw bright lights flashing in the distance. Maybe someone was coming for him... maybe he could go home. Blurred images of those he loved flashed before his eyes before they closed. Could it be they were real?

Chapter Six

Ralph's eyes opened and shut. Each time the flashing lights were a little closer. He was too tired and sore to move. The lack of food and water was taking its toll.

He heard voices in the distance. There was a certain amount of relief in knowing he recognized none. The man wasn't there. Ralph verified his conclusions with a sniff. The smell of smoke that constantly surrounded the stranger was absent. It was a smell he would never forget - no matter how long he lived.

A woman reached out. Ralph did little more than blink - what little focus he had left concentrated on her eyes. There was a kindness radiating from her expression, although mixed with sadness and concern. She was different from the man. Ralph knew in his gut she wasn't going to hurt him.

"Hello," she said. "I'm going to give you something for the pain. It will take a few minutes to work. You'll feel better soon - I promise."

A soft hand caressed the side of his face. He closed his eyes and soaked in all the compassion this woman was willing to give. He barely noticed the pin prick from an injection of medicine. At that moment he didn't care what it was, as long as she stayed by his side. A few minutes later and the pain subsided. Everything seemed surreal.

A dream. Maybe that was what this was. It was hard to distinguish. His senses failed him completely. He could make out nothing more than blurred visions and muffled noises. He felt like he was floating. There was no use straining. As long as the woman was with him, he was safe. If she was there, nothing else mattered. He drifted in and out of the realm of sleep.

26

Chapter Seven

"Ray," Sydney called out.

"Sweetheart," he replied, kissing her on the cheek. "What are you doing here? You should be resting."

"The hospital cleared me to come home," she replied, taking a step back from his cigarette. "Mother told me something happened to Ralph. I rushed right over. Is he okay?"

"I don't like the idea of you worrying. It isn't good for the baby. I'll take care of everything here and you go home and rest." He swung his arm around her shoulders, directing her back towards her car. "Everything will be fine." He inhaled deeply, taking in a lung full of nicotine.

She ducked under his arm, waving her hand in front of her face to clear the freshly exhaled smoke. "I'm not going to worry any less at home not knowing what is happening. If you won't tell me, I'm going in there to find out myself."

"Why do you have to be so stubborn?" Ray asked, ignoring her displeasure in his habit.

"I thought that was what you liked most about me," she teased. Taking a more serious note, she continued, "So, what happened? Why is Ralph here? Is he hurt?"

Ray sighed, running his fingers through his dark hair. "He attacked a boy."

"That's impossible," Sydney argued. "Ralph would never hurt anyone."

"Tell that to the boy's parents. I think it's time you admitted the facts," Ray said. "I've been telling you about his kind since the day we met."

"His kind?!" she echoed.

"I know you love him, but nothing you do or say is going to change the fact he is on the list for dangerous breeds of dogs," Ray replied, grabbing her arm to turn her away from the veterinary clinic. "I warned you it was only a matter of time before he snapped. It was bound to happen sooner or later. We are lucky you found out before the baby is born. Imagine how you'd feel if something happened to our child because of a dog."

She pulled her arm away from his grip. "He's family - my family! I know him. Your cigarettes are more danger to the baby than Ralph. Something must have happened to him." She dodged him and grabbed the door. "You promised me you'd quit."

"Fine!" Ray yelled, not wanting to cause a scene in front of witnesses. "There is nothing you can do in there." He flicked his cigarette butt into the street after using it to light a new one. "Don't worry about me quitting. I can stop anytime I want. I'll throw them away before the baby comes."

Chapter Eight

The veterinary clinic was empty except for a young woman flipping through some paperwork at the front desk.

"Hello," Sydney said, clearing her throat.

"How can I help you?" the woman asked without looking up.

"Um," Sydney started. If she hadn't known better, she would have thought she was in a hospital. The woman in front of her was dressed in green medical scrubs with her hair neatly tied back in a bun. A small name tag attached to a white doctor's coat read *Yen*.

The woman looked up, holding her gaze. "Yes?"

"My dog," Sydney started, her fingers fidgeting. "I understand he was brought in here last night."

The woman slammed her clipboard down on the desk. "So you're the owner," she barked. "If it were up to me, you'd be the one begging for your life not that poor animal."

"What?!" She had known Ralph was in trouble, but had no idea he could die. "Please," Sydney begged, "can I see him?"

"See him," The woman scoffed. "Haven't you done enough already? You should leave." She pointed to the door.

"Wait!" Sydney cried. "Can you at least tell me what happened to Ralph?"

Yen turned around. "You don't know?"

"No," Sydney answered. "I've had a hard pregnancy and was in the hospital until earlier today." Her hand instinctively rubbed her seven-and-a-half-month baby bump. "My mother told me there was an incident, but no one will give me details."

"Who was looking after him for you?" Yen asked.

"My future husband," Sydney answered. "We're getting married after the baby is born. He moved in specifically to look after Ralph while I was gone."

"Well, I'm sorry to have to tell you. A boy reported he was attacked by your dog."

"There must be a mistake," Sydney cried. "Ralph is a gentle dog. He'd never hurt a fly and definitely wouldn't bite a boy."

"There was no evidence of a bite from what I understand," Yen explained. "But the boy's parents are adamant your dog is a threat to the community. They have insisted on a formal hearing. Ralph's fate is in the hands of a judge now."

"Can I see him?" Sydney pleaded.

"I'm afraid not," Yen answered. "He's in quarantine at the moment. If you have a record of his shots, that would make things easier. You can ask the judge for visitation at the hearing."

Sydney rummaged through her purse, her hands shaking. "Here," she said, one hand emerging with a white card for Ralph's usual doctor.

Yen wrote down the information. "You better hold on to this. You may need a few character witnesses."

"Character witnesses?" Sydney echoed. "For what?"

"When we found Ralph, he was badly abused: a few broken ribs; malnourished; dehydrated; and neglected. It isn't just Ralph who will be on trial - someone will have to answer for animal cruelty."

Sydney gasped. This couldn't be happening.

Chapter Nine

The judge's mallet slammed down. "Silence," he bellowed. "Am I to understand you wish to end your engagement in my court room?"

"Yes," Sydney answered.

"You do understand this is a highly unusual request," The judge said, looking down at her over the top of a pair of round reading glasses.

She nodded, gulping back saliva that was pooling in her mouth and hoping no one noticed. She wiped the clamminess from her palms on the back of her dress.

"Very well, Miss Bennett," the judge said. "Bailiff, if you would please return the ring to Mr. Jorge."

"I object!" Ray yelled, sticking one finger in the air. He ignored his lawyer's pleas to sit back down.

"Object to what?" the judge asked.

"To Sydney returning my ring," Ray answered, quickly adding, "because of a dog."

The judge removed his glasses and rubbed his eyes. "Mr. Jorge," he said, "I am sure you are aware that this court has no jurisdiction on deciding if two people are to marry. If Miss Bennett does not wish to marry you, there is nothing I, or any other person, can do to change that. I simply cannot, nor would I want to, try to force this young lady to do anything she is adverse to doing."

The bailiff placed the ring on the table in front of Ray. He sat back down, letting out a huff. The red shade creeping into his face gauged his rising temper.

Sydney remembered his words. She was lucky to have found out before the baby was born - not about Ralph, but about the man she almost married. In a way, Ralph had protected her once again - this time from what very likely could have been the worst mistake of her life. He was a hero, not a villain. If only the judge could see that.

"He is a gentle dog," she blurted out. "The boy must have done something to provoke him."

"Please," the boy's mother said. "That dog is a menace to society. Justice needs to be served."

"He didn't bite," Sydney pleaded. "There was no sign of injury anywhere on the boy."

"Enough! I believe I have already heard all the evidence," the judge said. "Miss Bennett, I appreciate your position. This is, however, a court of law."

"Yes, your honour," she replied.

"Far too often do we expect we have the right to do anything we want," the judge explained. "Owning a dog is not our god-given right. It is a privilege. With privilege comes responsibility - in this case, responsibility to protect both the animal and the community. In that capacity both were let down. The question then becomes by whom."

Sydney rubbed her belly for comfort. A lump formed in the back of her throat.

"Miss Bennett is the lawful owner of the animal," the judge continued. "As such, she was responsible for making the proper provisions for him during her hospital stay. This Court finds that she had no reason to believe Mr. Jorge would not take proper care of her pet while she was hospitalized. As her future husband, she trusted him - appropriate behaviour for a woman in love. In light of this, all charges against her are dropped."

Sydney let out a sigh of relief.

"Mr. Jorge has admitted himself that he agreed to look after the dog while Miss Bennett was hospitalized. By doing so, responsibility to both the dog and the community were transferred to him. Therefore, this court finds him guilty of negligence and cruelty to animals. He is to be held for sentencing at the next

38

available date. Bail is set at two hundred and fifty thousand dollars."

"Are you mad?" Ray yelled as officers escorted him from the room.

The judge ignored his rants. "That leaves the issue of the animal. The dog in question is on the list of dangerous breeds. The law in this case is clear. Any animal on such a list who displays the ability for aggression is to be destroyed. While it is true that no blood was drawn this time, this court cannot guarantee the safety of others in the future. It is, therefore, my final decision that the animal be euthanized within twenty-four hours."

Sydney gasped for air. Tears streaked down her face, leaving black streaks from her mascara. "Please," she begged, chocking on the one word. Ralph had been her best friend since he was a puppy. Reality began to soak in.

"I'm sorry, Miss Bennett," the judge said. "The decision of the court is final."

She heard whispers of satisfaction from the boy's family members that justice was being served. Justice that involved taking the life of a member of her family. She cleared her throat.

"Can I at least be there with him?" she asked, forcing the words from her lips.

The judge nodded. "I have no problem with that request."

"Thank you," she whispered. For a moment, she thought she saw the glossy beginnings of a tear in the man's eye, but couldn't be sure it wasn't from her own blurry vision.

She plunked back in the hard wooden seat, waiting long after the rest of the courtroom had emptied before making her way outside to her car.

Sydney pulled a few tissues from her purse and used one to blow her nose - the other to clean up her face. She needed to be strong for Ralph. She would try not to let him see her cry.

Chapter Ten

One of Ralph's ears shot straight up. He knew that voice. A flood of memories rushed through his mind. It was her: in the bed cuddling with him; sitting at the table of food filling his plate; giving him a steak at the family barbeque; and raking the leaves into piles so he could jump in them and scatter them. That voice was his family. She was real and she had come for him.

The door squeaked open. Her familiar floral scent filled his senses. Ralph's tail moved as if it had its own mind - waving to the one who raised him.

"Hey, Ralph," she said, sitting on the floor.

It was an instant rush of adrenaline. For the first time since Ralph had come to this place, he felt alive again. He brushed against her hand, nudging for the attention that he had all but forgotten. Sydney rewarded him with scratches and kisses on the top of his head.

Kisses were his favourite. Ralph soaked in every single one and still wanted more.

"You're a good boy," she praised.

Ralph felt a drip fall on his head. He glanced up at her. *Tears.* He licked them from her face. This wasn't the time to be sad. This was the time to be happy. They were together again.

He let out a little yelp feeling a prick in his paw and pulled it away from the other lady. The medicine made him sleepy. He didn't want to sleep - not now. He wanted to love. He wanted to play. He was feeling young again.

His paw shook - it had lost feeling. He looked up at his family and snuggled. His eyes closed. He pushed them back open - fighting the hold sleep was taking in a losing battle. He sighed. His eyelids were becoming too heavy to force open anymore - no matter how much he wanted them to. Maybe a nap wasn't such a bad idea after all. He'd sleep for a little while and when he woke, he could go home with his family and play in the leaves.

The leaves. Jumping in the leaves would always be his favourite thing to do.

Chapter Eleven

Two weeks later...

Sydney wiped the sweat from her brow. Even though it was fall, there was absolutely no wind today. She sighed. There was no reason to complain. Without Ralph messing up the piles, she had finished the yard in record time, even taking necessary breaks for the safety of the baby.

She glanced at the small urn sitting on the picnic bench beside her. What was she thinking? Ralph was gone. He couldn't appreciate the leaves from where he was now. A tear formed in the corner of one eye before streaming down her face.

She glanced at the far corner of her property and shivered, remembering the day she came home and found the poor excuse for a dog house hidden behind bushes. It was gone now, but she still didn't understand how anyone could treat a dog like that.

Ralph had been such a free spirit. He loved life. He loved her. She missed everything about him.

A single leaf caught her attention as it cascaded down from above - gently floating onto the pile she had just finished racking. That leaf was like an epiphany. Without a single thought, she grabbed the urn and opened it. Ralph's ashes rained down on the pile.

Sydney shook her head. She must have been crazy. It was possible she had overworked herself. There were still weeks before the baby was due and rest had been ordered by the doctors. She propped the rake against the side of the house before opening the door.

Glancing back one more time, she smiled. The leaves that had been so neatly piled only a moment ago lay scattered across the lawn.

46

At that moment there was no doubt in her mind - Ralph had come home for one last romp in the leaves.

Author's Message

I hope you enjoyed Ralph's story. I did mention you might need a few tissues - I know I did while writing it.

You may have noticed that I didn't mention in this story where it was taking place or which breed of dog Ralph was. Perhaps you already figured this out, but it is because it could happen anywhere and to any breed of dog on any number of lists.

While Ralph is a fictional character, his story is lived by many every day. Each of us has the power to change the ending. If you see an animal in need, please call your local authorities or SPCA, or take a moment to learn the facts about breed specific legislation in your area. You can make a difference in an animal's life.

Thank you for reading! If you enjoyed this story, please browse through some on my other titles currently available.

The Portal Prophecies

These great titles in C.A. King's The Portal Prophecies series are available now at most online book retailers:

A Keeper's Destiny

A Halloween's Curse

Frost Bitten

Sleeping Sands

Deadly Perceptions

Finding Balance

The prophecies are the key to their survival. Can they solve them in time?

Tomoiya's Story

A Vampire Tale. She had a secret, but she wasn't the only one with something to hide.

Escape to Darkness

Collecting Tears